THIS BOOK BELONGS TO

The Legend of

THE WHISTLE PIG WRANGLER

by Kate Allen

Illustrated by Jim Harris

The Kumquat Press

To my little wranglers, Lauren, Jamie, and T.J.

SPECIAL THANKS TO

Lauren, Ted, Wilma, James S., Susie, Jeff, Diane, Marion, Jim, Lorie, Joanne, Michael, Kem, Kathy, Karen, Reed, Jim B. and Jenny Sue.

The Kumquat Press, 3790 Via de la Valle, Del Mar CA 92014
Design and Production by Albion Publishing Group, Santa Barbara, California
FIRST EDITION
FIRST PRINTING, 1995
ISBN 1-887218-00-9
Library of Congress Catalog Number 95-79690
The Legend of the Whistle Pig Wrangler by Kate Allen; Illustrations by Jim Harris – 1st edition
32 pages
Summary: A southwestern tale of courage and determination

Manufactured in Hong Kong

WHAT'S A WHISTLE PIG?

A whistle pig is a small animal called a marmot (mar-mut). Members of the squirrel family, their cousins include the prairie dog and the chipmunk.

These furry creatures make their homes among the rocks and boulders on mountain slopes.

Very alert and wary critters, they are famous for the shrill alarm whistle they sound to warn others of danger. Most of their day is spent sunning, grooming, and digging for roots and plants.

LONG, LONG AGO in Castle Rock, Colorado, where the mountains bulge and the air is clean, lived a little whistle pig named William.

Every morning, dressed only in his long johns, William jumped from his bunk, grinned at himself in the mirror and whistled the tune,

"HAPPY TRAILS TO YOUUUUU, KEEP SMILING UNTIL THEN."

In fact, William whistled all day long. Some say he even whistled in his sleep.

With great detail, this cowboy outfitted himself for the day: a pair of green suspenders to hold up his pants, a knotted bandana to keep his neck warm and dry, and leather chaps fastened tightly around his legs.

The "jingle jangle" of the silver spurs always tickled his heart, when he pulled his boots up close to his knees. And on wet and windy days, he never forgot to wear his yellow slicker.

His tall Stetson® was the last thing he added. Well, that and the big smile that came over his face.

Early every day William grabbed a bunch of carrots and raced to the barn. "Mornin', Pinto Bean," he would say. "How ya' doin'?"

William brushed this critter till he shone like a polished apple.

He took great pride in grooming his horse. Someday soon this would be a wrangler's mount.

When William slung the saddle blanket across Pinto's back, his heart beat like an Indian tom-tom.

With the gear all in place, it was time to hit the trails.

Day after day William and Pinto Bean rode up the winding mountain slopes and down into the deep canyons.

They often stopped at Beaver pond. The locals loved William's rendition of "Whistle While You Work," and worked harder than ever, though, they never did figure out how to whistle.

William's whistling, mixed with the beaver's gnawing, and the occasional "SNAP, CRACK, BOOM," from a falling tree, made for quite a woodland symphony.

As they circled the ridge, the smell of the pine and the fragrance of the early spring snow made William happy to be alive. "Oh, Pinto Bean," he'd say, "isn't it a wonderful day."

William practiced his riding and roping with great determination. He wanted more than anything else, to be a real live wrangler.

With his lariat close at hand, William chased his friends all over the mountains.

The deer and bunnies, however, had different ideas about whistle pig wranglers. . . and especially their flying lassoes. They preferred to play hide-and-seek.

One day, William was riding through the junipers, whistling at the top of his lungs, when he smelled something funny. It was a prickly kind of scent. Pinto Bean smelled it too. Then he felt it.

OOOuch!!!!

Poor Pinto, quills stuck on his bottom, bucked and kicked all the way back to Castle Rock.

When the commotion was over, all the townspeople had scurried for cover—except for the mayor, who was found clinging to the top of the flagpole.

'Most always, William managed to look more dignified when he came to town. Sitting tall in his saddle, William would gallop down Main Street, tip his hat to the ladies and shout, "HOWWWWWWDY!"

One time, William and Pinto Bean trotted into town just in time to see a runaway stallion.

"WHOA! Look at that Cavvieyah (kav' ee-yah). He's out of control!" yelled William. "Come on, Pinto Bean, let's get him!"

William seized his lariat and hurled it with a mighty force.

"WOOOOOps!" said William to Pinto Bean.

When the dust settled, it took three deputies to untangle the sheriff of Castle Rock.

The day came when William arrived at Pinto Bean's stall, and he was not whistling. There was a serious look on his face. "Pinto," he announced, "today is the day of the Castle Rock Roundup—the biggest of the whole year."

Pinto Bean perked his ears forward.

"And Pinto," whispered William, "WE'RE going, too!"

Sure enough, when the Castle Rock Wranglers rode out of town that morning, there were William and Pinto Bean, right at the end of the line; that is, until the trail boss turned around in his saddle and saw them.

"You trailin' us son?" he called gruffly. "Git on home. This ain't no whistle pig picnic. It's real wrangler work!"

With a lump in his throat that felt like a pine cone, William could hold the tears back no longer. A great big, salty, drop rolled over the end of his nose, all the way down to the tip of his rawhide boot.

Just then, something caused the hairs all over the little whistle pig to stand on end. His nose twitched. He scanned the horizon, and he smelled it. So did Pinto Bean!

"Vamoose (va-moose')," shouted William.

Their noses led them straight to the edge of Coyote (ki-o' te) Canyon. Pinto Bean slid to a stop. His ears flattened, his nostrils flared, and his hooves pawed the ground.

"What is it Pinto?" asked William.

There was something wrong, terribly wrong!

William first spotted them in the chaparral (chap-ar-ral').

Coyotes under the pinons. Coyotes behind the sagebrush. Coyotes hiding everywhere, hundreds of them. The ravenous scoundrels drooled as they eyed their next meal.

"OH! NO!" shouted William. "An ambush!"

Throwing back his head, he tried desperately to whistle. But nothing came out, not even one little gasp of air.

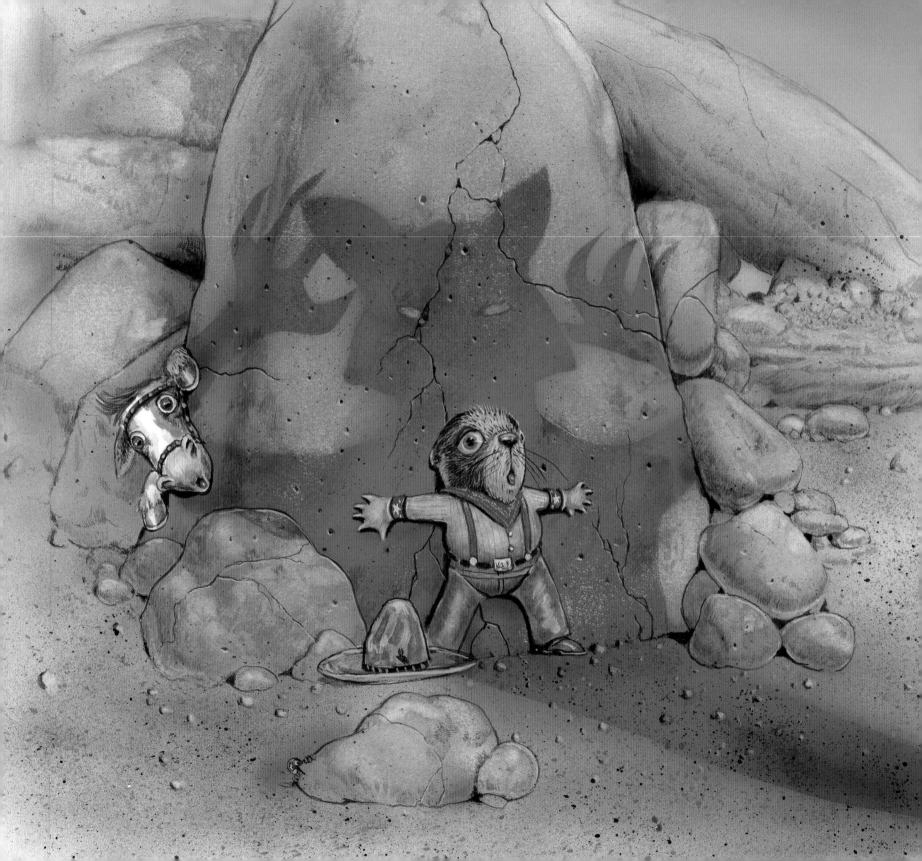

Closer and closer the coyote gang crept, sneaking through rabbit bush and around huge boulders.

Frozen to the ground, William trembled. Pinto Bean scrambled behind William and shook. Then the biggest, meanest coyote turned and headed straight for William and Pinto Bean.

Reaching way down to the bottom of his lungs, William sounded the loudest and most piercing whistle of his life.

His bandana flapped wildly as the air exploded from his throat. Pinto Bean jumped ten feet.

The coyotes "HOWWWWWLED" and "HOWWWWWLED" and ran away like they were caught in a prairie fire.

Down below, the cattle threatened to stampede, and the wranglers clasped their hands over their ears. The trail boss kicked his horse into a dead run up to the top of the canyon. "What's goin' on up here?", he yelled at William.

Still whistling, William could only point.

The sight of the retreating coyotes and the shrill sounds coming from the whistle pig provided the cowboy with all the clues he needed.

"Lemme shake your hand, partner!" he boomed. "Only one kind of "hombre" (ohm'bray) could've saved us from them coyotes. . . .," he paused as William's last whistle echoed through the walls of the canyon. "And that's a real live wrangler!"

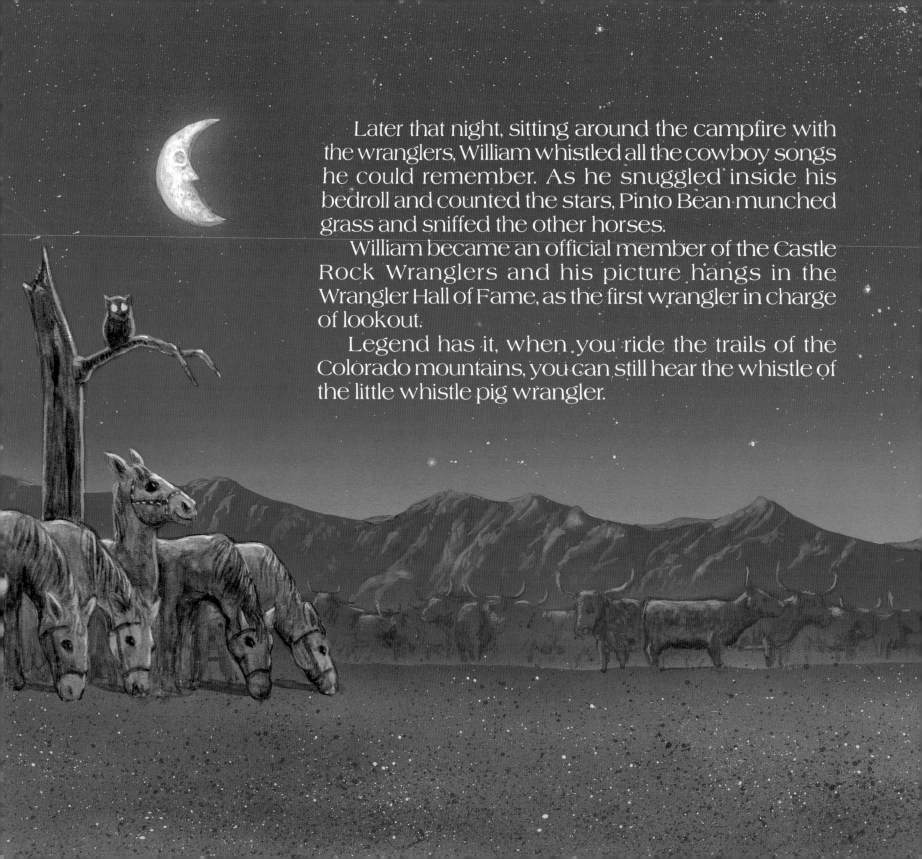

Later that night, sitting around the campfire with the wranglers, William whistled all the cowboy songs he could remember. As he snuggled inside his bedroll and counted the stars, Pinto Bean munched grass and sniffed the other horses.

William became an official member of the Castle Rock Wranglers and his picture hangs in the Wrangler Hall of Fame, as the first wrangler in charge of lookout.

Legend has it, when you ride the trails of the Colorado mountains, you can still hear the whistle of the little whistle pig wrangler.

COWBOY LINGO

AMBUSH To hide and attack by surprise.

BANDANA A brightly colored scarf worn around the neck for protection from dust, sleet and bitter wind.

BEDROLL A bed for under the stars made of rolled blankets, and frequently used as a place to stash a cowboy's belongings.

BUNK A narrow bed with or without a double deck.

CAVVIEYAH (Kav'ee-yah) A cowboy's way of saying the Spanish word *Caballo*, which means horse.

CHAPS Flaps of leather worn around the leg to protect a cowboy from cattle horns, chaparral, rain, and horse bites.

CHAPARRAL (chap-ar-ral') An area of dense brush or small trees often used as a hiding place for wild animals.

COYOTE (ki-o'te) A dog-like wolf that attacks small animals as well as livestock.

CRITTER Can mean any animal.

GEAR The saddle, bridle, rope, and other items used by the cowboy.

HOMBRE (ohm'bray) The Spanish word for "man".

LARIAT A cowboy's rope.

LASSO A rope with a loop at one end used to catch horses and cattle.

MOUNT An animal to ride.

PINTO A horse with two colors.

PRAIRIE FIRE A fire on an open range. This was a big fear for cowboys and animals, for if it was not stopped it could destroy everything in its path.

LONG JOHNS The cowboy's underwear.

ROUNDUP The herding of cattle or horses to a place to brand, count or sort them.

SADDLE BLANKET A blanket put between the saddle and the horse's back.

SLICKER A coat made of oiled canvas used not only to protect the cowboy from the elements but also as his suitcase.

SPURS A metal implement with a spiked wheel attached and worn around the boot. It was used not to hurt the horse but to give him an extra prod.

STAMPEDE A cowboy's nightmare. Animals running wildly out of control, usually due to fright.

STETSON®* The original Stetson hat was made by John B. Stetson in 1863 to cover the head from the sun, rain, and snow. Everyone laughed at first. However, after selling thousands of hats, Stetson came to mean a cowboy's hat.
*Stetson® is a registered trademark of the John B. Stetson Company.

TRAIL BOSS A man in charge of a herd of cattle or horses.

VAMOOSE (va-moose') From the Spanish word *vamos*. It means "Let's go" or "Let's hit the trails".

WRANGLER A cowboy who handles horses. During roundups he usually wrangles five to nine extra mounts.

KATE ALLEN, AUTHOR

Kate Allen lives on a ranch in Southern California, where she raises one husband, one daughter, three horses, seven dogs, eight birds, four chickens, two bunnies, two ducks, one turkey, and a ranch hand named Donald. Having taught kindergarten for several years, she has a deep respect and love for children and animals. Kate's nine year old daughter is an avid horsewoman and provides her with much inspiration. Kate is currently writing a book for women and several other children's books.

JIM HARRIS, ILLUSTRATOR

Best known for his humorous illustrations of children's books, Colorado illustrator Jim Harris brings to his art experience with clients as diverse as National Geographic Special Publications, The Danbury Mint, and Sesame Street. During his thirteen years as a freelance illustrator, first near Chicago and now in rural Colorado, Jim's illustrations have appeared on greeting cards, posters, magazines, calendars and collectibles as well as children's and young adult titles. Many of Jim's illustrations have won awards, among them the Silver Medal from the Society of Illustrators' Annual Exhibition and the Certificate of Merit from Communication Arts.